A Baseball Giant

Lee Aucoin, *Creative Director*
Jamey Acosta, *Senior Editor*
Heidi Fiedler, *Editor*
Produced and designed by
Denise Ryan & Associates
Illustration © Mark Jones
Rachelle Cracchiolo, *Publisher*

Teacher Created Materials
5301 Oceanus Drive
Huntington Beach, CA 92649-1030
http://www.tcmpub.com
Paperback: ISBN: 978-1-4333-5644-5
Library Binding: ISBN: 978-1-4807-1743-5
© 2014 Teacher Created Materials

Written by
Nicolas Brasch

Illustrated by
Mark Jones

Contents

Chapter One

A Present to Remember

Eiji loved baseball. He carried his ball and glove with him everywhere. He played baseball every day during lunch at school. Then, he played it every day after school. On weekends, he played for the local team, the Kita Aces.

On his tenth birthday, Eiji's dad gave him an old wooden box.

What a strange present, thought Eiji, but he didn't say that to his dad.

"This box belonged to your grandfather," Eiji's dad told him. "Before he died, he asked me to give it to you on your tenth birthday."

Eiji still had strong memories of his grandfather. As he opened the lid of the box, he remembered how much he had loved him. And he knew how much his grandfather had loved him.

Inside the box was a baseball, a crumpled piece of paper, and some black-and-white baseball cards.

5

"These are very special," Eiji's dad said.

"I know. They belonged to Grandad."

"Yes, and some of the cards are of his hero, the greatest Japanese baseball player of all time," Eiji's dad explained.

"Who?"

"Eiji Sawamura. You were named after him." Eiji had always wondered why his parents had named him Eiji. Now he knew.

How cool, Eiji thought. *I'm named after the greatest Japanese baseball player of all time!* Eiji looked through the cards and found one of Eiji Sawamura. He peered at it closely, trying to see if he looked like his namesake.

"What was he like?" Eiji asked his dad.

Eiji Sawamura

Chapter Two

The Americans Arrive

Eiji's dad had waited many years to tell this story. But he started by asking Eiji a question. "Who do you think was the greatest American Major League baseball player of all time?"

Eiji didn't hesitate. "Babe Ruth."

"And the second best?"

"Lou Gehrig." No question there.

"And have you heard of Jimmie Foxx and Charlie Gehringer?"

"Of course, they're legends."

"Well, Eiji Sawamura was the pitcher who struck them all out!" his dad explained. Eiji was dumbstruck. "And he was only seventeen at the time," his dad added.

"But where? When?" Eiji had to know more.

"It was back in 1934. Eiji Sawamura was a seventeen-year-old schoolboy at the time. A team of American Major League players came to Japan to play a team of Japanese players."

"Were they from the Japanese Major League?"

"No, this was just before the Japanese Major League was formed."

"They came from teams all around the country. And Sawamura was selected because he was thought to have a lot of promise as a pitcher."

Already, Eiji liked what he was hearing. He had a feeling that he was going to be proud to be named after Sawamura.

Eiji's dad continued. "The first seven games in the series were easily won by the American players. There wasn't a professional league in Japan, so it didn't seem like a fair contest."

"Did Sawamura play in any of those games?" Eiji asked.

"No. But he did play in the eighth game. He didn't start, but they brought him in to pitch at the beginning of the fourth inning."

Chapter Three

Four in a Row

Eiji's dad continued the story. "Few
people in the crowd had heard of Sawamura,
and none of them expected him to change
the game. He stepped up to the mound
after warming up his right arm. He batted
left handed but pitched with his right hand."

"Just like me," Eiji broke in.

"Yes, just like you," his dad smiled. "For the next five innings, Sawamura pitched the game of his life! He struck out Charlie Gehringer, Babe Ruth, Lou Gehrig, and Jimmie Foxx all in a row."

"Wow!" Eiji tried to imagine such an amazing streak.

"The fans couldn't believe what they were seeing. And they weren't the only ones. Along with the American players, there were officials from some of the American Major League teams. They began to imagine what this young ballplayer could do for their teams."

"Did he sign with any of them?" Eiji wanted to know.

"Be patient. I haven't finished the story."

"Sorry."

"For five innings, Sawamura threw against the best players in the world. He threw just one bad pitch, and Lou Gehrig hit it for a home run. That was the only run scored the entire game. The Japanese team lost 1-0, but the result didn't matter. Eiji Sawamura had shown that he was ready for the big time."

Eiji took in all that his dad had told him. *No wonder Sawamura was my granddad's hero,* he thought. He looked again at the collection inside the box. He looked closely at the piece of paper. It was hard to make out the characters, but his dad helped him.

"That's Sawamura's autograph!" Eiji exclaimed. "Whoa!"

Chapter Four

The No-Hit Legend

Eiji's dad continued his story. "Several American Major League teams tried to sign Sawamura, but he refused. There's even a story that he signed a contract with one of the teams by mistake."

"By mistake?" Eiji asked?

"Yes, they gave him a piece of paper. He thought he was just signing an autograph, but it turned out to be a contract. When he discovered what he had done, he told them that he didn't mean to sign the contract and would not go to America."

"So, what happened next?"

"Two years after his game against Babe Ruth and the others, the Japanese Major League was formed. Sawamura joined the Yomiuri Giants and became the star of the team—and the league."

Eiji looked at one of the baseball cards with Sawamura's picture on it. "It says here he threw three no-hitters."

"That's right. He pitched three games without any player on the other team ever hitting a ball and reaching first base."

"That's incredible!"

"Your grandfather saw him play. But no one knew it would be his final game." Eiji's eyes widened and his father continued. "He was forced to go to war in 1943. The following year, the ship he was on was hit by a torpedo, and Sawamura was killed."

"That's terrible!" Eiji exclaimed.

"In war, no one is spared. No one is special," Eiji's dad said as he shook his head.

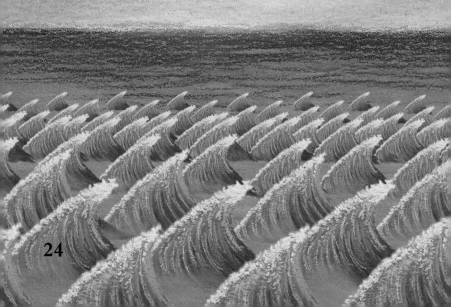

Chapter Five

On the Mound

The next day, Eiji had practice. He warmed up with his team. He usually pitched relief for the Aces, but today his coach tossed Eiji the ball and said, "You're up first."

Eiji threw a few balls to the catcher to warm up his arm. He felt different. He felt more confident. He didn't feel nervous at all.

"Batter up!" the umpire called.

The first batter walked to the plate, took a couple of practice swings, and got into position. Eiji stared at the batter, wound his arm back and pitched—straight into the catcher's glove.

"Strike!"

Again, the batter got into position. Eiji pitched. *Thud!* Straight into the catcher's glove.

"Strike!"

The batter looked nervous. He got into position again. Eiji took a deep breath. He could see his granddad in his mind, smiling. He could see Eiji Sawamura in his mind, nodding encouragingly.

"Zero and two," the umpire called.

Eiji pitched. The batter swung. *Thud!* Into the catcher's glove again.

"Strike three!"

As the first batter walked to the bench and the next batter came to the plate, Eiji felt strong. Today was going to be a good day.

31

Nicolas Brasch lives in Melbourne, Australia. He is a highly regarded writer of children's nonfiction and fiction books. Several of his books have won Australian Educational Publishing Awards. Nicolas also wrote *Hot Springs and Brown Bears* for Read! Explore! Imagine! Fiction Readers.

Mark Jones was born in Switzerland, grew up in Florida, graduated from the School of Visual Arts in New York City, and currently lives in London, England. Mark has illustrated many children's books. He also paints beautiful murals. Mark also illustrated *Escape from Pacaya* for Read! Explore! Imagine! Fiction Readers.